A bumping, a thumping–I've heard it before.

Feet on my carpet and claws on my door!

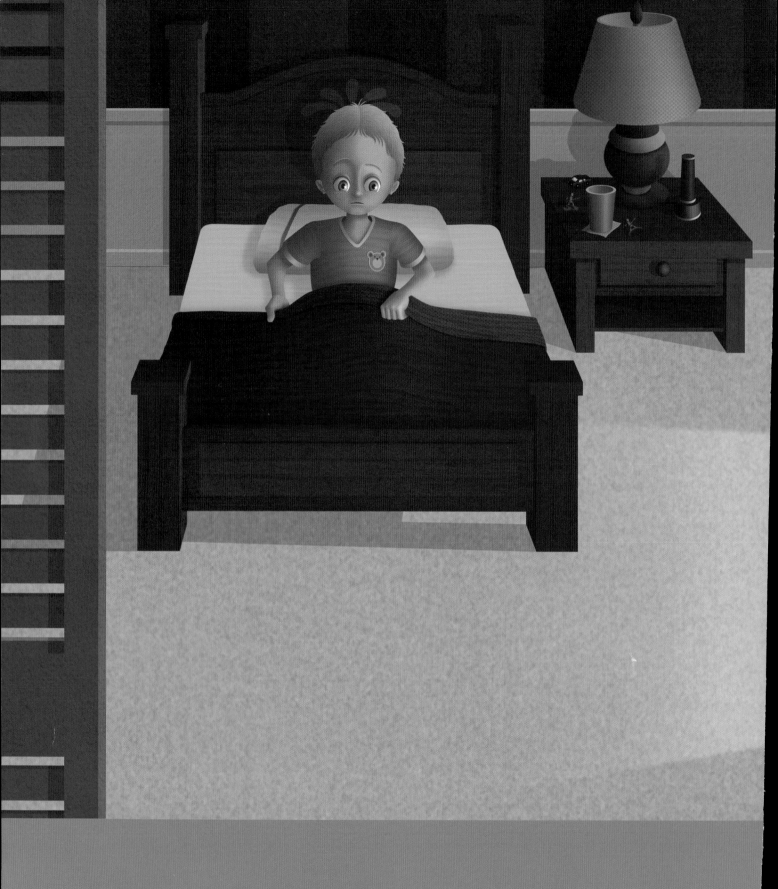

A *baddie*, a *beastie*, a *banshee*, a *blight*,

A *ghoulie*, a *ghostie*, a fuzzy green *fright*!

A *creeper*, *grim reaper*, a sneaky *trespasser*,

A foul-smelling *terror*, a night-time *harasser*!

It's scaly and hairy, all tangled and bumpy.

It's stinky and slimy and probably grumpy.

With one crazy eye and a horn with a mole,

A big, spiky *gremlin* who walks like a *troll*.

Just then!

Did you hear it?

It *must* be ...

I'm certain!

It came from that drawer
or from
behind the curtain!

Get out of here, Monster!

Scat!

Scram!

Skedaddle!

At once leave my room or to Mommy I'll tattle!

She'll be here in
seconds. She's
on her way now!

She really hates
monsters who
grumble and growl.

She'll find where you're hiding and how you got in.

She'll first reassure me, and then we'll begin.

We'll shine a light on the nooks and the crannies–

Open my closet and pull out my jammies.

Out of the shadows and into the light,

Run away, Monster, out into the night!

And last, but not least, just one final measure–

This little black bottle is something I treasure.

I'll get out my Brave Spray, and then you will see

Monsters like *you* don't scare brave kids like *me*!

For in this small bottle, a magical blend

Keeps *monsters* away and helps me defend.

It's made from the things that *monsters* fear most!

It smells just like oranges and Daddy's French toast.

Monsters and *meanies* and *ogres* BEWARE!

With good smells like these, you can't breathe the air!

I'm going to sleep now. My room is protected.

Good dreams are coming, bad *monsters* rejected.

Remember! At night when you creep near my bed

A brave kid like *me* will scare *you* instead!

For my Little Monsters, Finn & Matthew

And with special thanks to Chase & Sophie for contributing your artwork.

TALKING TO YOUR KIDS ABOUT MONSTERS

Nighttime can be a scary time for children. At ages 3-8, their imaginations are developing, and during this time children have trouble differentiating fantasy from reality. When children wake from a nightmare, they are afraid of the monsters they saw as real, living things. Recurring nightmares can make bedtime very scary. In your role as a parent-guardian, it is critical that you model strength and reassure them you will keep them safe, but not belittle their fears. This is an opportunity to teach your children bravery, taking action in the face of adversity. It is a lesson that can help them through all the challenges they will endure. Tips for dealing with your children's fears & creating a more comfortable bedtime environment can be found on our website, at: **www.monster-defense.com/bedtime**

Monsters Beware!
Copyright © 2014 by Matthew W Hardesty
Library of Congress Control Number: 2014903273
ISBN 978-0-9912130-0-9

Monster Defense Corp.
PO BOX 23032, Lincoln, NE 68542-3032.

Additional information, including our full line of products at **www.monster-defense.com**

Printed in the United States of America by

Redbrush

1201 Infinity Court, Lincoln, NE 68512
(#052014)